This book belongs to:

_____

A catalogue record for this book is available from the British Library

Published by Ladybird Books Ltd
80 Strand, London, WC2R 0RL
A Penguin Company

2 4 6 8 10 9 7 5 3 1
© LADYBIRD BOOKS LTD MMIX
LADYBIRD and the device of a Ladybird are trademarks of Ladybird Books Ltd

ISBN: 978-140930-242-1

Printed in Italy

My Storytime

Hannah Hippo's New Helper

written by Ronne Randall
illustrated by Jill McDonald

Deep in the jungle, there was a winding, wandering river. It was the glubbiest, blubbiest, *muddiest* river anywhere.

Perfect for hippos!

Hannah Hippo and her friends *loved* the mud! They played games like...

kick splash...

8

mud paddle...

and even deep-mud diving!

9

No matter how hot and steamy the jungle was, the mud was always nice and cool.

In fact, the only things that ever made the hippos hot were the buzzing, nipping insects that flew around the river.

Luckily for the hippos, the friendly birds who lived around the river thought the insects were delicious. Each bird chose its favourite hippo and sat on its back quietly feasting on bugs and flies.

12

So most of the hippos were very happy. All except one.

Poor Hannah didn't have her own bird friend to eat up all the bugs!

"This buzzing and biting and itching and twitching is driving me mad!" said Hannah. "I'll have to find a friend of my own!"

15

So Hannah set off up the river.
Soon, she met Carl Crocodile.
"Hello, Hannah," said Carl Crocodile,
snapping his shiny white teeth. "I'll help
you to get rid of those biting bugs!"

"No, thanks," said Hannah,
swimming past as fast as she could.

Hannah swam further up the river.
"Hello, Hannah!" shouted Lewis Lion
and Thomas Tiger. "We'll help you to
swish those nasty flies away with our tails!"

"No, thanks," said Hannah,
swimming quickly by.
"That won't work for me!"

Soon, Hannah was in a part of the jungle she'd never seen before. She was a little bit scared.

"Maybe I'd better go home, before I get lost," she thought.

But, suddenly, Hannah heard something in the trees. It was a little bird.

21

Hannah waved to the bird, and the bird fluttered down and settled on her tummy. The bird picked and pecked hungrily, and soon all the bugs were gone!

Before long, Hannah was swimming happily home with her new friend on her back.

"No more itching or twitching!" thought Hannah. "Thank you, Little Bird!"

"Tweet!" cheeped Little Bird.

"Welcome home, Hannah!" called her friends. "We thought you were lost. Where have you been?"

"I've been all the way up the river," said Hannah. "And I've found a new friend."

"Tweet!" said Little Bird.
Hannah knew what
that meant…

She had her own special bird
friend at last. And no more itches!